WHAT WE
LIKE TO DO

WRITTEN BY

Monica Ittusardjuat and Kathy Knowles

My name is Utak.
I live in Nunavut.

I like to go to school.

I like to eat country food.

I like to play in the snow.

10

My name is Peace.
I live in Ghana.

I like to go to school.

I like to eat corn.

I like to play in the sand.